LITTLE MISS SPLENDID
SPLENDID
and the house with a view

Original concept by Roger Hargreaves
Illustrated and written by Adam Hargreaves

D1635507

MR. MEN   LITTLE MISS

Little Miss Splendid looked out of her very splendid window, set in her most splendid house, at her very splendid garden and smiled.

And then she frowned.

Little Miss Splendid looked out of her window every morning and every morning she smiled and then she frowned.

And what made her frown?

I'll tell you.

At the bottom of her garden on the other side of a small stream lived Mr Mean.

Unlike Miss Splendid's very large and most splendid house Mr Mean's house is very small and very run down.

A not at all splendid house.

In fact, the most un-splendid house one could ever imagine.

Mr Mean was the sort of person who did not like spending money, especially on his house.

Little Miss Splendid was the complete opposite.

And she did not like having Mr Mean as a neighbour.

His house quite ruined her splendid view.

It was on this particular morning as she stood looking out of her window that Miss Splendid had an idea.

She rang her builder, Mr Trowel.

"Hello," she said, "This is Miss Splendid. I would like you to build a wall for me. Come at once."

Mr Trowel was over within an hour and within a day he had built a wall at the bottom of Little Miss Splendid's garden.

A high wall.

A wall that hid Mr Mean's house.

Now, Mr Mean also liked to look out of his window each morning.

He had a splendid view of Miss Splendid's extraordinarily splendid house.

And what made the view all the more splendid for Mr Mean was the fact that it hadn't cost him a penny.

Mr Mean was very unhappy when he looked out of his window the next day and all he could see was a high, red brick wall.

But as he stood there looking out of his window Mr Mean had an idea.

The next morning when Little Miss Splendid looked out of the window she couldn't believe her eyes.

There was a huge hole in her beautiful wall and through the hole she could see Mr Mean's ramshackle house.

Miss Splendid was furious.

She rang Mr Trowel immediately and by lunch-time Mr Trowel had rebuilt the wall.

But the next morning there was another hole in her wall.

And so it went on all week.

Overnight Mr Mean would knock a hole in the wall and the next day Mr Trowel would come and repair it.

And then one morning the whole wall had disappeared.

But not just the wall.

There was no sign of Mr Mean's house either!

"That's strange," said Miss Splendid to herself. She put on her best hat and went to investigate.

When she got down to where Mr Mean's house had been she heard the sound of building coming from the other side of the hill. She climbed to the top of the hill.

And for the second time she couldn't believe her eyes.

There was Mr Busy putting the finishing touches to a house that looked liked hers, but was even more splendid!

"Looks good doesn't it?" said a voice behind her.

It was Mr Mean.

"What ... what ... how?" spluttered Miss Splendid.

"It was all those bricks that gave me the idea," said Mr Mean and grinned. "All those free bricks!"

Little Miss Splendid didn't know what to say.

So she didn't say anything.

And she went home.

To her splendid house.

A splendid house, but no longer the most splendid house!

3 Great Offers for MR.MEN Fans!

MR. MEN TOKEN

1 New Mr. Men or Little Miss Library Bus Presentation Cases

A brand new stronger, roomier school bus library box, with sturdy carrying handle and stay-closed fasteners.
The full colour, wipe-clean boxes make a great home for your full collection.
They're just £5.99 inc P&P and free bookmark!

☐ MR. MEN ☐ LITTLE MISS (please tick and order overleaf)

2 Door Hangers and Posters

In every Mr. Men and Little Miss book like this one, you will find a special token. Collect 6 tokens and we will send you a brilliant Mr. Men or Little Miss poster and a Mr. Men or Little Miss double sided full colour bedroom door hanger of your choice. Simply tick your choice in the list and tape a 50p coin for your two items to this page.

PLEASE STICK YOUR 50P COIN HERE

Door Hangers (please tick)
☐ Mr. Nosey & Mr. Muddle
☐ Mr. Slow & Mr. Busy
☐ Mr. Messy & Mr. Quiet
☐ Mr. Perfect & Mr. Forgetful
☐ Little Miss Fun & Little Miss Late
☐ Little Miss Helpful & Little Miss Tidy
☐ Little Miss Busy & Little Miss Brainy
☐ Little Miss Star & Little Miss Fun

Posters (please tick)
☐ MR. MEN
☐ LITTLE MISS

3 Sixteen Beautiful Fridge Magnets – any 2 for £2.00! inc.P&P

They're very special collector's items!
Simply tick your first and second* choices from the list below
of any 2 characters!

1st Choice
- [ ] Mr. Happy
- [ ] Mr. Lazy
- [ ] Mr. Topsy-Turvy
- [ ] Mr. Bounce
- [ ] Mr. Bump
- [ ] Mr. Small
- [ ] Mr. Snow
- [ ] Mr. Wrong
- [ ] Mr. Daydream
- [ ] Mr. Tickle
- [ ] Mr. Greedy
- [ ] Mr. Funny
- [ ] Little Miss Giggles
- [ ] Little Miss Splendid
- [ ] Little Miss Naughty
- [ ] Little Miss Sunshine

2nd Choice
- [ ] Mr. Happy
- [ ] Mr. Lazy
- [ ] Mr. Topsy-Turvy
- [ ] Mr. Bounce
- [ ] Mr. Bump
- [ ] Mr. Small
- [ ] Mr. Snow
- [ ] Mr. Wrong
- [ ] Mr. Daydream
- [ ] Mr. Tickle
- [ ] Mr. Greedy
- [ ] Mr. Funny
- [ ] Little Miss Giggles
- [ ] Little Miss Splendid
- [ ] Little Miss Naughty
- [ ] Little Miss Sunshine

*Only in case your first choice is out of stock.

CUT ALONG DOTTED LINE AND RETURN THIS WHOLE PAGE

--- TO BE COMPLETED BY AN ADULT ---

To apply for any of these great offers, ask an adult to complete the coupon below and send it with the appropriate payment and tokens, if needed, to MR. MEN OFFERS, PO BOX 7, MANCHESTER M19 2HD

- [ ] Please send ____ Mr. Men Library case(s) and/or ____ Little Miss Library case(s) at £5.99 each inc P&P
- [ ] Please send a poster and door hanger as selected overleaf. I enclose six tokens plus a 50p coin for P&P
- [ ] Please send me ____ pair(s) of Mr. Men/Little Miss fridge magnets, as selected above at £2.00 inc P&P

Fan's Name _____

Address _____

_____ **Postcode** _____

Date of Birth _____

Name of Parent/Guardian _____

Total amount enclosed £ _____

- [ ] **I enclose a cheque/postal order payable to Egmont Books Limited**
- [ ] **Please charge my MasterCard/Visa/Amex/Switch or Delta account** (delete as appropriate)

Card Number

Expiry date ___ / ___   **Signature** _____

Please allow 28 days for delivery. We reserve the right to change the terms of this offer at any time but we offer a 14 day money back guarantee. This does not affect your statutory rights.

MR.MEN   LITTLE MISS
Mr. Men and Little Miss™ & ©Mrs. Roger Hargreaves